Dedicated to Scott, Will, and Anika Anderson
(the author's grandchildren)
and to Maggie who really wrote her own story.

D1219244

With special thanks to John 'Jo' Anderson
for his encouragement and support.

Maggie's in the wagon;
She can't believe her eyes.
She thought she would be left behind
When the sun began to rise.

The children wave at Maggie.
Maggie smiles and wags her tail.
She'd like to stop and get a pat,
But off to Maine she sails.

Maggie sees the traffic,
The buildings, trees, and flowers.
She stops sometimes to stretch her legs,
Then rides along for hours.

Maggie is a traveling dog.

Maggie Goes to Maine

Written by
Betsey Anderson

Illustrated by
Thomas Block

Maggie Goes to Maine
Copyright © 2013 Betsey Anderson
ISBN 978-1-938883-83-5

Illustrations by Thomas Block

Designed and produced by
Maine Authors Publishing
12 High Street, Thomaston, Maine 04861
www.maineauthorspublishing.com

Printed in the United States of America

Maggie sees the mountains,
The lake, the fields, the woods.
She sees a fox, a skunk, a deer;
She'd jump out if she could!

Maggie is an excited dog!

Maggie keeps on smiling;
She never does complain.
It's clear by now that Maggie knows
She's finally in Maine.

Maggie is a patient dog.

Maggie's getting anxious.
She can't wait to explore.
While everyone unpacks the bags,
She slips out through the door.

Maggie is a curious dog.

Maggie smells the daisies,
The clover, and the hay.
She rolls around in buttercups
And hears a noisy jay.

Maggie is a busy dog.

Maggie hears a rustle
And whips around to see.
A mouse gives Maggie quite a chase,
But finally ends up free.

Maggie is a dizzy dog!

Maggie races to the lake.
A duck sees Maggie there.
She quacks and quacks and leads her from
The ducklings in her care.

A nosy goose is watching
Within the reeds nearby.
It sounds as if it might be fun—
He wants to add his cry.

The duck, the goose, and Maggie—
What a noise they make!
A **quack**, a **splash**, a **honk, honk, honk**;
No quiet at this lake!

Maggie is a silly dog!

Maggie's in the woods now,
Beyond her family's call
It's getting late; the sounds are strange,
And what's this? Something tall!

Maggie's eyes get bigger.
She stops short at the sight.
She's seen all kinds of cats and dogs,
But not a moose at night!

Maggie is a frightened dog.

Maggie's heart starts pounding.
She runs away so fast,
And all at once she knows she's lost
And suppertime has passed.

Maggie is a sad dog.

Maggie finds a farmhouse
And scratches at the door.
Perhaps these folks will help her out;
She's hungry and she's sore.

They bring her in the kitchen
And give her a warm meal.
Then next they call the constable.
They know how she must feel.

He'll take her back to camp soon;
He puts her in his truck.
Maggie's very happy now.
 His name is Mr. Buck.

Maggie is a lucky dog!

Maggie knows she's leaving.
She's had a lot of fun.
But now it's time to say good-bye
To Maine's blue sky and sun.

Maggie is a good dog.

Maggie gazes out the window
For one last loving peep,
Then quietly lays down her head
And goes right off to sleep.

Maggie is a tired dog.

About Maggie:
Maggie's favorite thing to do was to swim in Webb Lake while her best friend Sam, an older beagle, watched from the canoe.

About the Author:
BETSEY ANDERSON is from Dixfield, Maine, and lives in Chapel Hill North Carolina with her husband John Anderson. They return every summer to the Elsemore family camp in Weld. A very special place!

About the Illustrator:
THOMAS BLOCK retired as an art educator in coastal Maine after 37 years to pursue a career as an artist/illustrator. His recent books include *Togus a Coon Cat Finds a Home* by News Center 6 Don Carrigan and *Baxter in the Blaine House* by Blaine House director Paula Benoit. Thomas has illustrated several young adult novels as well, including *Patch Scratching* by Steven Powell, and *The Black Ledge* series by Paige W. Pendleton. Thomas lives and works by the sea in Midcoast Maine.